E
WIE
Wiest, Robert   C.2

There's one in every
bunch

Child Coll

Child Coll

DATE			

© THE BAKER & TAYLOR CO.

There's One in Every Bunch

By Robert and Claire Wiest

 CHILDRENS PRESS, CHICAGO

To our parents, Gerda and Bill,
Grace and Andy, without whom none
of this would have been possible

Library of Congress Catalog Card Number   78-159786

2 3 4 5 6 7 8 9 10 11 12 13 14 15 16 17 18 19 20 21 22 23 24 25 R 75 74 73 72

Owls...

on a limb...

in the forest,

don't just give a hoot.
They bark
  mew
  groan
  cluck
  hum
  chatter
  squeak
  toot
  whistle
  yelp
  coo
  cough
  rattle
    and hiss.
They live in borrowed homes

in short trees,

in tall trees,

in old trees,

and in palm trees.

But one shares his home

with a

woodpecker

in a cactus.

Most owls are shy.

In the daytime they hide

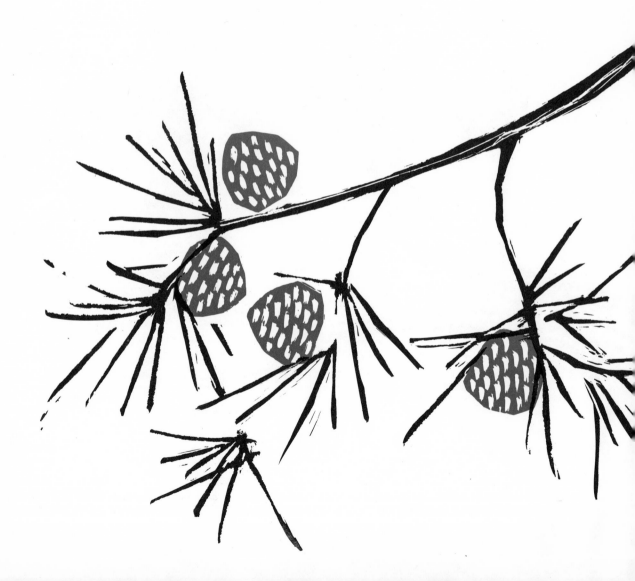

in pine forests,

in rain forests,

in leafy trees,

in barn lofts,

and in church steeples.

But there is one who

claps his wings

and flies over meadows

in the bright sunshine.

In the nighttime owls are bold hunters.

They have large eyes and sharp beaks.

They catch snakes,

lizards,

moths,

mice,

and bats.

But not all owls like to hunt.

One would rather go fishing.

There's one

in every bunch—

or two—

or more.

Robert and Claire Wiest are natives of Massachusetts. Claire was graduated from Massachusetts College of Art in 1953 and has painted professionally ever since. She is best known for her work in watercolors and graphics, and has received many awards in these media. Her work is included in public and private collections in the United States, Canada, Sweden, and Finland.

Robert Wiest attended the University of Massachusetts and served four years in the United States Coast Guard as a radioman. During subsequent years in industry, he became more and more interested in writing, printing, and bookbinding. In 1968, he and Claire set up the Bark River Press in Delafield, Wisconsin, where they hand produce limited editions of books and cards. Many of the ideas reflected in their work come from the fields, hedgerows, and streams near the tiny community of Delafield, where they live with their teen-age son.

Here again the author-artist team, who did *Some Frogs Have Their Own Rocks,* bring us a glimpse of life from their nearby woods in an economy of line and a minimum of text.